25 Ways to KEEP Your Man…
Or
Re-gain His Love

By: *Heather Hetheru Miller*

25 Ways to Keep Your Man:

...Or Re-gain His Love

Copyright © 2020 by Heather Miller
Published and distributed in the United States by:
Heather Miller * Heathermiller1988@gmail.com
Detroit, MI * (313) 759-7855

Edited by:	**Cover Designed by:**
A'Rita Young-Parks	Heather Hetheru Miller

DEDICATION

This book is dedicated to my husband Calvin for his patience and commitment as I continue to find new ways to love and value him.

ACKNOWLEDGMENTS

A special thank you to all of the men who contributed their stories, experiences, thoughts, and feelings to build this book. For believing that women can be retooled with the "good" information to understand his love language and bring peace to their relationships.

25 Ways to Keep Your Man... Or Re-gain His Love

This book is a companion to:

"100 Ways to Keep Your Woman... or Re-gain Her Love."

Women! We have become such creatures of habit so entrenched in media materialism and fantasy that we have forgotten how to communicate, humble ourselves, love, and find our peace. I pray this tool be a blessing to you as you re-create, re-store, or re-assess yourself and your relationship with your partner/mate.

Men often complain that most women carry emotional baggage from previous relationship into committed relationships. They point out that some women want to take the leadership role of a man in their relationship; that she talks (more fusses) more than listen; that she changes in her level of intimacy; that she sometimes invest too much in her "processed" look (weave; make up) or invest very little in her appearance (stretch pants, jeans, jogging pants; little grooming and hygiene). He doesn't have to have a beauty queen; but he does want a queen; to stand beside him (as king).

They share that women complain, argue and fuss instead of communicate with logic. They believe this limited style of communication comes from bitter previous relationships or the expectation that their partner/mate is their "girlfriend" and will respond as another woman would. This vicious cycle of bitterness and brokenness must end if peace and love will prevail in our committed relationships.

We all are born and endowed with the skills for successful

relationships. We are also capable of unlearning and reassessing ourselves so we aligning with who and what we want.

Many of us pray and have prayed to God to give us who we want and what we need; when the truth is... we may not be ready to get what we asked for!

In any important endeavor there is a plan, preparation, implementation, execution, and reflection process. Within this process, the more you practice, the better the results! There are spiritual laws and practical strategies that can translate this process into successful relationships.

The first important endeavor is to know YOU. Not just the "you" that you dress up every day often in a mask acceptable to the public eye (but damaged in our own) not the "you" pretending that its always someone else who is at fault when they are often reflecting back to YOU what you may not see in yourself....

This is the "You" who is undergoing a process to be and become whole.... better... stronger... kinder... peaceful... forgiving... patient... beautiful! The woman who stops men in their tracks because they "feel" the peace and power radiate from within you...

This woman is the woman who will value and appreciate "25 Ways to Keep your Man... **AND** Regain His Love."

1) **Remember men are problem solvers first**! They listen to "fix" the problem for you. They are not listening as the kind ear of a girlfriend would!

   INSIGHT! Limit unnecessary or excessive girlfriend chatter!

   Share the tangible problems that he can fix!!! Or limit your "idol" chatter to 3-5 minutes!

   REFLECTION NOTES:

2) **Remember your man is a HERO**! By design, he is programmed to rescue his fair maiden!

INSIGHT! Let him rescue You! Don't deny him the rights of manhood. Yes you may be able to fix a tire but do you really want to? NO!!!! let him fix the tire and save the day!

REFLECTION NOTES:

3) **Men are emotional** and often insecure… just like women. However, they have been conditioned, groomed, and prompted to "suck it up" don't show emotion or vulnerability (often by women and society). It is often seen as a sign of weakness and weakness is an invitation to be judged, used and hurt!

INSIGHT! Allow him to put his guard down with you both in public expectations and private domain at home. In public affirm his manhood stand with him not in front of him! Do not speak for him, apologize if you are wrong or overstep your boundaries. Remember he has lived and survived a good number of years without you and can survive many more without you… but why let him get away?

REFLECTION NOTES:

4) **You are NOT his mother!** He already came out of that portal and away from those apron strings (for the most part).

INSIGHT! Do not confuse "nurture" with "nature"! To nurture is knowing his mental, physical, emotional needs and creating a safe space to share in it with him. Nature is the natural bond between mother and child; it is often blameless and if focused; will supersede you or your expectations and judgment. Eventually it will leave you without a whole or present man. **BE HIS LOVER NOT HIS MOTHER!**

REFLECTION NOTES:

5) **Set, assess and represent a personal and spiritual standard!** Hold yourself to standards not seeped in materialism and expectations of others. Live by your truth to the best of your ability and understand why you don't have or have not yet mastered a standard. Strive for it daily. BE an example that he can model, affirm and emulate.

INSIGHT! Be consistent. Show him you are a woman of standards so that he has a standard to uphold as well. This helps him be a better person too! Talk the talk and walk the walk!

REFLECTION NOTES:

6) **Don't be so "churched" that you forget where the "Spirit of God" dwells.** God should not only be worshipped by the gathering of the congregation but at the fellowship of the family. Many men are "turned off" or discouraged by the church and other religious systems by their experiences and the types of people it produces. Praise and worship is present in your attitude of gratitude and should always be in your words, acts and deeds.

INSIGHT! Live your beliefs at home, at work and in your relationships so that the true principle of your belief can be lived by you both and both expect and benefit from the blessings of your belief.

REFLECTION NOTES:

7) **Be mindful of your tone, words and delivery** of your

comments while communicating. You are two

capable adults and the basics of any healthy

relationship is communication!

INSIGHT! Speak in quiet, hushed tones. Do not yell or

verbally abuse or name call. Use your tone to RESPECT

your mate or partner. Leave the manners of the "world

outside" and bring to your shared space and

environment of mutual respect.

REFLECTION NOTES:

8) **Be mindful of his "triggers".** These triggers can be words, body language and facial expressions. He will always forewarn you of his triggers if you are listening. When he says "I hate when ….." Even if it is a reference to a past relationship or loved one… Listen and take heed!

INSIGHT! Do not antagonize him! Read his body language so as not to push him into a corner where his triggers are forced causing him to behave in a common manner as done in the past. Don't push, be quick to apologize and reassure him with a gentle touch and "hushed" tones.

REFLECTION NOTES:

9) **FEED him!** All healthy bodies need food... The healthier and better tasting the happier and healthier he is. When you increase fresh citric fruits and a combination of mixed colored vegetable it cleanses his digestive system, blood and all bodily fluids making them "taste" better.

INSIGHT! Prepare meals with love and raise your vibration of the foods you serve him. Pray over them while selecting, cooking, and eating your meal. This also raises the vibration and enhances the flavor and aroma of the food.

REFLECTION NOTES:

10) **SPEAK life over him and into him!** This simply

means to use positive, loving and affirming words

that build him up and encourage your relationship.

INSIGHT! Complement his strengths, gifts, abilities,

good manners, solutions, insights, ideas, intelligence,

and his experiments to improve himself. Affirm him in

the areas he may be insecure especially in his standing

as a man, lover, father, friend, employer/employee,

leader, son, etc.

REFLECTION NOTES:

11) **BE silent!** Spend more time listening than talking. If he has a glossed over look in his eyes you have likely gone too far! Pull back ask him about his thoughts without putting him on the spot with your "vagina monologue" your females problems, curiosities, and venting moments) talking incessantly; non-stop.

INSIGHT! Test him and find out how much chatter he can take after 3 -5 minutes. Typically, beyond 5 minutes of chatter you lose him (at least your attention span).

REFLECTION NOTES:

12) **Give him some space!** Gauge what he needs when

he first comes home. Watch what he does if he

immediately steps into relaxation mode let him. Do

not bring bills, problem, conflict, confrontation

without giving him a 30 minute delay.

INSIGHT! Do not give him a shopping list of problems to

sort and solve. Share the top 2 most pressing and

gradually integrate those of importance with a sit down

and talk request later in the day. If it can wait, keep it.

REFLECTION NOTES:

13) **Know what makes him feel at home.** Is it a favorite chair? Drink? A kiss or hug? Time with the kids? Ask and observe. His past relationships and upbringing can be clues!

INSIGHT! Make him feel at home. Home is his sanctuary. His family serves him at home as he serves the world outside. It means go above and beyond to affirm his comfort, control and love in this space.

REFLECTION NOTES:

14) **Learn how to manage money!** This is a deeper

matter of trust in his mind!

INSIGHT! Money management has to do with

responsible choices and discipline. Talk through the

issues before they become a problem and work together

toward solutions. Remember he wants/needs to fix

problems. By working together and planning solutions

to get through the challenge, doing it together, builds

your relationship.

REFLECTION NOTES:

15) **Be MINDFUL of your habits and vices**. They can

sometimes lead to unhealthy confrontations.

INSIGHT! Keep yourself in check. If you know your

habits disturb him, begin the process to eliminate or

reduce them. The most aggravating vices that men

notice in their women are smoking, talking loud,

arguing, challenging his authority, untidy home, poor

money management, gambling, too much time with/on

the phone, social media, or with friends, excessive time

spent outside of the home, constant criticism, poor

hygiene, flirting, being ungrateful and poor manners.

When you know; let it go!

   REFLECTION NOTES:

16) **Keep an open mind to his backstory** (family values, experiences). This will help you understand him as he seeks to be understood and not criticized for past choices/decisions.

INSIGHT! Know his backstory but do not hold it against him by bringing it up during arguments as leverage. The information should be to help you avoid passed pitfalls and preserve him and his feelings. You should have enough information to protect him and increase his trust and security.

REFLECTION NOTES:

17) **Demonstrate and maintain honesty in communication**. Do not LIE to him! It is better to gently address the issues than to have to lie to cover up things you didn't want to share or disclose. When you begin to lie, you will eventually lose track of the previous lies told/used to cover up the previous lie. Talk through your issues before it become a bigger problem.

INSIGHT! Honesty is more difficult for some than others. Our bigger issue in honesty is fear of loss. We are often afraid of losing the trust, the faith, the admiration/love of our partner. Remember there are issues that occur prior to the lie that is brewing. Think through your choices carefully.

REFLECTION NOTES:

18) **Speak in HUSHED tones!** Mind your manners,

volume, and tone. He is a man of equal value and

equal respect; not a child that you reprimand and/or

constantly correct!

INSIGHT! Check your emotional responses. Typically,

when a woman gets emotional and angry she is often

more verbal and chatty, her voice gets loud, her words

become more sarcastic and condescending, and her

tone has and aggressive or annoyed attitude. Do a

frequent self check!

REFLECTION NOTES:

19) **Use good MANNERS!** Say please, thank you, excuse me. These 3 phrases carry more weight in demonstrating respect than you know.

INSIGHT! Good manners are expressed in conversation too. So instead of interrupting him while he is speaking, say "excuse me" to show him value and respect. Instead of bumping him and keep going, say "excuse me"!

REFLECTION NOTES:

20) Give him generous amounts of praise!

INSIGHT! Acknowledge and celebrate milestones at work, with the kids, with you! BE thankful for what he does and his show of effort. Let it stand alone without adding the word "But…" as it negates anything said before it.

REFLECTION NOTES:

21) **Be 3 times the woman** as is hoped for and expected!

INSIGHT! Be his wife! Be a patient, encouraging, giving and forgiving...

Be his friend! Be understanding, supportive and listen...

Be his lover! Stimulate all of his senses, know his value, build his confidence!

REFLECTION NOTES:

22) **Do not manipulate** him or insult his intelligence to

get your way.

INSIGHT! Remember he has lived a full life and has

many experiences. Also note that HE also has intuition

and instincts that when alerted, will raise his awareness.

Manipulation always cause harm to others that

ultimately returns to you. Act out of your honesty and

build and maintain trust.

REFLECTION NOTES:

23) Do NOT put any other man before him!

INSIGHT! Be mindful that "any" man could include your

son, pastor, boss, male friend or any other man who

wants more attention than entitled or than you should

give him.

   REFLECTION NOTES:

24) **Know that his compliance does NOT mean weakness**!

INSIGHT! Compliance is a form of submission; this level of submission is based on trust. Trust and the re-establishment of trust will be key to changing and shifting your relationship for the better.

REFLECTION NOTES:

25) Fight the urge to "SHUT DOWN"!

INSIGHT! Be still, stay present and listen before reacting. When you use the phrase "Nothing" when you get angry is a form of manipulation. You are really hoping that he will keep pushing you to say what you really wanted to say. When, if you are that upset, you should simply say that "I am upset or my feelings are hurt right now. Can you give me a few minutes to collect my thoughts and we can talk more later." COMMUNICATE! Then when you do calm down, ask him if it's "okay" to talk about what was bothering you earlier.

REFLECTION NOTES:

WISDOM & Quick Recap of 25 Ways…

As you recap and reflect on the identified 25 ways to love him, just know that there are truly UNLIMITED ways to love him that you can ADD TO this basic list. It's important not to skip this list! The WAYS shared in this guide come directly from men during focus groups, research studies and even barbershop talk. The range of men that contributed input were from ages 28 – 68. They were single, dating, non-committal, committed, married, separated, divorced and the very special category of "I'll NEVER do that Sh*t again". They wanted us to dig a little deeper into the qualities that have meaning for them. In the pages following you will see the deeper insights that might help you navigate additional ways to love him or regain his love.

Remember men are problem solvers first!

1. Remember your man is a HERO!
2. Men are emotional
3. You are NOT his mother!
4. Set, assess and represent a personal and spiritual standard!
5. Don't be so "churched"
6. Be mindful of your tone, words and delivery
7. Be mindful of his "triggers"
8. FEED him!
9. SPEAK life
10. BE silent!
11. Give him some space!
12. Know what makes him feel at home.

13. Learn how to manage money!
14. Be MINDFUL of your habits and vices
15. Keep an open mind to his backstory
16. Demonstrate and maintain honesty in communication.
17. Speak in HUSHED tones!
18. Use good MANNERS!
19. Give him generous amounts of praise!
20. Be 3 times the woman
21. Do not manipulate
22. Do NOT put any other man before him!
23. Know that his compliance does NOT mean weakness!
24. Fight the urge to "SHUT DOWN"!

Make sure to use the space set aside for your reflection notes. Use it to review your initial reactions and thoughts to the 25 ways listed within the book.

Think about your how, when, and why you may need to consider adding each tool to <u>your</u> healthy relationship tool box!

BONUS: <u>MUST HAVE</u> TOOLS & WISDOM FOR THE JOURNEY…

You may have picked up this book and thought, "I already do those things" or "Why should I have to do all of this? He's the one that…" This is exactly why, you need this book and these complimentary tools and wisdom! You NEED new information to get a NEW result from your relationship! READ ON!

TOOL #1: THE PROCESS OF CHANGE...

There are *steps* to change. Change is *created* through YOUR action. Changing your attitude and mind-set doesn't happen overnight. But if you want your relationship to work, this is a great place to start. Consistency is key! The steps to change are:

- *New Information*

- *Appreciation of the information enough to use it*

- *Application of the new information to your situation*

- *Transforming your mindset to think and be a new way*

- *Elevating to the new and more lovable YOU*

TOOL #2: CHANGING OLD HABITS FOR A NEW LIFESTYLE TAKES TIME

Change is a process and the process takes work and time. Once you recognize the behavior and/or value that you want to change and you identify the new behavior that you want to replace it with, the REAL work begins. Begin applying your new behavior for 7-10 consecutive days. This is the beginning stages of your change where it becomes a replacement to old habits. Continue the new behavior for a consecutive 21 days and you will see that it become easier to do because the habit is more real and intentional. Keep it up for 3 consecutive 21 day cycles (that's 63 days) and it will become your lifestyle. This strategy works with most things you look to change. In relationships behavior shifts and it is essential that you stay consistent. If you miss an opportunity take a deep breath, forgive yourself and begin again (at your day one) until you reach your 10 days. Celebrate your efforts!

TOOL #3: WISDOM OF WOMEN OF DIVORCE....

There are many women who take advantage of a good man (thinking him weak, believing he may lack the qualities of the "man of their dreams", believes he is mistrustful, or may label him as out-right incompetent) and are now reaping the harvest of the ill-treatment they have sown when he finally has decided that he has had enough!

Typically, this bitterness (on her part or his) comes from a vicious cycle in previous relationships, dishonest intentions, lack of honesty and often unhealthy levels of manipulation. He may or may not be the victim of the crimes of love, lust, and possession but often all of us must own some of the responsibility of what has happened to/in our relationships. No one is a totally INNOCENT victim in love. Relationships are three-sided (You, Me & the Truth). But in healing old wounds and beginning new beginnings, YOU have to take aggressive steps if you are going to preserve your relationship and re-gain his love.

You can recover from divorce... and he can recover from divorce! But you must spend the time listening, reflecting and admitting to the complaints and reasons that your previous mate gave for their unhappiness in the relationship. Then look at your parents and their relationship. Do you see what your mate saw in you too? There may be some truths for you to assess in this observation. Because we are both part of our each parent we may also have reflective tendencies as we reach their age/stage of relationship.

TOOL #4: DON'T LOSE A GOOD MAN FOR YOUR LACK OF

PATIENCE!

Just because he doesn't respond to you as you may have hoped...

Just because he is not "superman" in bed...

Just because he is not wealthy...

Just because he is not in the best physical shape...

Just because he is sensitive...

Doesn't mean that with the right type of loving and support he can't become the type of man you want and need! He may need a reset and YOU may be the one who really needs to change.

Here is your self-check:

1) Do you criticize or scrutinize him more than 1 time per week?
2) Do you "tell" him what to do or "make" requests/ask him for consideration?
3) Do you raise your voice during conversations?
4) How often does he "shut down" and/or refuse to talk to you a day?
5) How many times have you turned down his affections or rejected him in bed?
6) How often do you laugh? Hug? Kiss? Say I love you per day?

Do you see where this Self-Check is going? You may have some blame in the state of your relationship.

TOOL#5 THE SIGNS AND SYMPTOMS OF A GOOD MAN?
These are the 10 signs that you have a GOOD man:

1) He practices his faith and answers to God.
2) He is honest.
3) He comes home.
4) He occasionally brings you a gift (food, date nite, something you like)
5) He remembers important dates (doctor's appointments, anniversaries, birthdays).
6) He asks about the people who are important to you.
7) He contributes to helping around the house.
8) He is willing to listen and will even consider what you share.
9) He wants to do his part to provide for you and his family.
10) He talks to you about decisions.

TOOL #6: THE TOP 5 RELATIONSHIP RESTORATION CURES:

1) You must WANT to make it work.

2) You MUST be willing to extend MORE effort to demonstrate your willingness to change.

3) YOU must apologize and tell him where YOU have made mis-steps in the relationship.

4) You MUST bring God into your relationship by taking the issues to God first to resolve and look within you for the problem and solution.

5) You MUST increase the amount of affection and praise that you give to him.

TOOL#7: REMEMBER WOMEN ARE PROCESS-ORIENTED, FEELING AND CHATTY!

Do not expect him to be a woman! You must approach him with logic and not emotion! If he is more emotional than you, then creating balance in your relationship is key. The answers are in his backstory.

TOOL #8: A MAN WON'T TRUST A WOMAN WHO WILL NOT MEET HIS PHYSICAL/SEXUAL NEEDS.

Men are very physical and up and through to middle adulthood (45 – 65), are sexually active and/or sexually interested. Rejection and denial of sex/sexual stimulation is an immediate turn off with a long-term impact that often influences his virility and confidence. Find creative ways to engage in sexual activity and physical contact.

TOOL #9: REMEMBER THAT MOST MEN ARE TASK-ORIENTED, LOGICAL, AND PROBLEM SOLVERS!

If you deny him enough times (the support and right to fix things) he will lose interest in fixing things for you... but he will FIX something for someone else who will appreciate his fixing!

TOOL #10: MEN ARE VISUAL CREATURES.

He is attracted by what he sees. He does like to see a woman who looks feminine. He recognizes the difference between sexy and sensual. Sexy is temporary; Sensual is long-term. While women look fabulous in long hair (i.e., weave, processed), revealing all in tight pants, revealing clothes, and push up bras (implants, padding, and spanks), he ultimately does like to see and see himself settling down with a natural woman (with good hygiene and manners).

TOOL #11: MEN LIKE YOUR NATURAL BEAUTY.

While women think make up, wigs/weave, and body gear make us the ultimate sex symbol or show us as flawless, men think to the contrary. They would rather know that who they see and meet will be the same person who they wake up with the next day and into the future.

TOOL #12: HE WANTS TO TOUCH YOU.

Men want affection not rejection. He also wants to be touched. Reaffirmed. Desired. Appreciated. Teach him how to love you so you can get the love you need to give him the love he needs!

TOOL #13: REMEMBER PEOPLE CHANGE IN RELATIONSHIPS.

As long as people are growing on and growing up, they are

changing. Every role we settled into takes time to "grow up" in.

There is infancy, middle age, and seasoned stages of our roles as

mate and partner. No one was born a husband, wife or parent.

There are instincts that prompt our basic needs. We look to our

own parents for examples. We look to our culture and society for

ideas and expectations (that we often find in the media) for the

roles we play. We get angry when our partner falls short, reveals

that they were "faking it until they make it", is confused, didn't

have good role models and finally admits their truth; that they are

ready to live in this new reality of a relationship. Remember

change can be good when its built upon a good foundation!

IN CLOSING…

THANK YOU!!!

Thank you for choosing 25 Ways to Keep Your Man or Regain His Love. The greatest advise that I can share with you that supersedes all that you have read, is to keep your center in God, and create a space of peace within and without (inside of you and in your environment). I pray that your heart and mind has been opened to "see" your mate or partner. RESPECT him. Celebrate him. Rebuild your relationship with him with new information and new tools to secure a lasting reality.

If you are seeking additional tools, you may also be interested in other "Lessons for the Journey" books, resource, and tools like blogtalks, articles, workshops, lessons, and YouTube videos found under your search for Heather Hetheru Miller, Personal Change Coach. Google me or reach out at heather2hetheru@gmail.com with your feedback and comments. Visit www.yourinspiredjourney.com for more information on workshop, sessions and upcoming events. "…*Be transformed by the renewing of your mind…" Romans 12:2*

"Let the Journey Continue…."

Heather Hetheru

###